Strong...and...free...

strong...

and Free...

written and illustrated
by
Amy Hagstrom

LANDMARK ℒℰ EDITIONS, INC.

1420 Kansas Avenue, • Kansas City, Missouri 64127
(816) 241-4919

Dedicated to
My mom and dad,
and my pony, Chief

Second Printing

COPYRIGHT© 1987 BY AMY HAGSTROM

International Standard Book Number: 0-933849-08-7

International Standard Book Number: 0-933849-15-X (LIB.BDG.)

Library of Congress Cataloging-in-Publication Data
Hagstrom, Amy, 1976-
  Strong and Free.
  Summary: With the help of an Indian friend and through his own love and
understanding of the wild Appaloosa ponies, a young boy finds the courage to
save the herd from horse thieves.
  [1. Appaloosa horse—Fiction.   2. Horses—Fiction.
  3. Robbers and outlaws—Fiction.   4. Friendship—Fiction.]
  I. Title.
  PZ7.H12457St   1987   [Fic]   87-3942

Editorial Coordinator: Nancy R. Thatch
Creative Coordinator: David Melton

Printed in the United States of America.

STRONG AND FREE

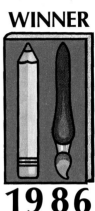

In the judging of THE 1986 NATIONAL WRITTEN & ILLUSTRATED BY... AWARDS CONTEST FOR STUDENTS, Amy Hagstrom's book, STRONG AND FREE, posed a problem. Because the text was so skillfully written, it was difficult for some judges to believe it had been written by a nine-year-old.

After reading the first few pages, readers will understand why the judges were so impressed. The narrative skillfully transports readers to another time and place, introduces the characters with ease, and interjects dialogue with a grace that lets us live the story. Amy also has a complete sense of chapter construction and development.

Amy's style of illustration is of great interest to me. In order to develop impressionistic moods and scenes, she cuts stencils and uses sponges to apply the color. Her placement of the images and the colors is very mature. And her choices of where to apply detail and how much she should leave to the viewer's imagination create visual delights.

After Amy won the 1986 Contest in the age category of 6 to 9 years, she told me she had been afraid her book wouldn't win, because she wasn't "good at art." When she asked me if I would teach her to draw, I told her, "not for this book."

I did only one thing to help Amy improve her illustrations. When I saw that she had cut her stencils out of construction paper — which absorbs moisture and wrinkles out of shape when wet paint is applied — I bought her some stencil paper. Then I left her on her own to compose her final illustrations. My choice was a proper one indeed. As you will see, Amy's illustrations are perfect for the mood of her story.

— David Melton

Creative Coordinator
Landmark Editions, Inc.

Chapter 1

Billy and the Ponies

His mighty legs trembled. His shiny red coat sparkled in the sunlight. As he tossed his head and sniffed the wind, his bright eyes searched all around. Several other ponies galloped by, but there was no doubt — this great Appaloosa stallion was the leader, just as his ancestors had been leaders a hundred years before.

A twelve-year-old boy sat on the rocky bluff overlooking the meadow and watched the ponies graze. He knew that in years past, the Nez Perce Indians had raised the Appaloosas to be strong, fine ponies.

The ponies were beautiful, with shiny coats of red and blue. Their wide heels made them surefooted on rough ground, and because their forefeet turned in, they could delicately tiptoe along the narrowest pathways. And they were also very fast — faster than any other horses on the plains.

But there was something unusual about this wild herd of Appaloosas — something mystical that Billy could not explain. Maybe the red and black spots that shimmered and glistened on their coats gave them a magical look. Or maybe the boy was just imagining things.

In the late afternoon, Billy climbed down from the bluff and started back toward his family's ranch. As he walked, he continued to think about the ponies. He didn't know a lot about the Appaloosas. But he was sure that if these magnificent creatures were ever in danger, he would want to help them.

As Billy unlatched the gate, he heard his father's voice.

"Billy! I've been looking for you. Did you go to the meadow again?"

"Yes, Pa," Billy replied.

"Well, you'd better get our horses rubbed down and into their stalls."

"Yes, Pa," the boy repeated.

As Billy rubbed down a mare of auburn color, he wished he could ride her. But that wasn't allowed, because she belonged to his father. All the same, Billy pictured himself on her back, with her legs galloping full stride. His daydream was suddenly interrupted by the sound of his mother's voice.

"Billy, supper's ready!" she called.

When Billy walked into the kitchen, he saw a familiar visitor standing by the fireplace. It was Concha, his best friend.

"Hi, Concha!" Billy said, and smiled at the man.

"Hello, Billy," Concha answered.

The old Nez Perce Indian's skin was dark and wrinkled, and his hair was snow white. He stood tall, his back straight as a ramrod. And his dark eyes were clear and direct as he looked at Billy.

Billy and Concha had been friends for a long time. Billy admired his wise friend. The old Indian had taught Billy many things. He had taught him how to ride a horse bareback, how to fish, and how to track wild animals.

Concha had told Billy the story of what had happened to his family long before — of how white soldiers had driven them off their land and forced them to live on a reservation. Many of his tribe had died. And those who survived hated having to live on the reservation.

In the kitchen, the smell of fried chicken and gravy filled the air. Tonight everybody ate and talked about the day's events.

As soon as Concha finished eating, he said, "I must go. Thank you for the food."

"Must you leave so soon?" Billy asked.

"Yes," replied Concha, "but I will not be far away. I will see you soon."

The next morning, Billy awoke and dressed quickly. After he fed and watered the horses, he asked his father if he could ride Ginger, one of the family horses. As soon as his father said, "Yes," Billy ran to the stables and climbed onto Ginger's bare back. One nudge with his heels and the little black mare cantered toward the meadow.

The Appaloosas were still there, and they didn't seem to mind Billy riding so close to them. The ponies acted like they trusted the boy. Billy climbed down and stretched out on his stomach on the grass. He leaned his face on his hands and watched the ponies intently. Then hearing a noise behind him, Billy turned and was surprised to see Concha standing before him.

Chapter 2

The Indian Legend

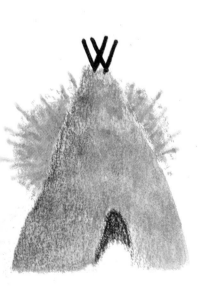

"For many days, I have seen you watch the ponies," Concha said. "Now that we are alone, I want to talk to you about them."

"Sure," Billy replied, "I think they're wonderful horses."

"Yes, they are," Concha said quietly. "Have you ever heard the old Nez Perce legend about the Appaloosas?"

"No, I don't think so," Billy answered.

"A long time ago," Concha said, "a tribe of Nez Perce fought a great battle with white soldiers, not far from this meadow."

"Really?" Billy exclaimed.

"It is true," Concha nodded. "The white men wanted the great herd of Appaloosas, because these ponies were so strong and fast. The fierce battle lasted throughout the day. And the white men were winning, but the Nez Perce would not surrender. They were ready to die.

"Then at sundown," Concha continued, "from out of nowhere, many Appaloosa ponies appeared. As they galloped toward the center of the battle, their hooves thundered against the earth.

"The white soldiers were astonished. They could not believe their eyes. They watched in amazement as the Appaloosas formed a circle around the Nez Perce and led the tribe to safety in a nearby canyon."

The old Indian paused and his eyes looked far into the distance.

"The white soldiers followed," Concha said, "but once they were inside the canyon, they could not find the Indians or the Appaloosas. They were puzzled, because there was only one way into the canyon and one way out."

"But where did they go?" Billy asked eagerly.

"Some people think there is a secret pass leading out of the canyon," Concha answered, "but no one has ever found it."

"Gosh!" Billy exclaimed.

"The Nez Perce believe the Appaloosas saved the tribe," Concha said. "The ponies in this meadow are descendants of those horses, so my people believe they are sacred. But times are changing, and now I worry about the Appaloosas."

"But why are you worried?" Billy wanted to know.

"Each fall the Appaloosas leave their home in Utah and travel to a warmer place in Arizona," Concha explained. "In early spring, they always come back. In years past, we Nez Perce held a ceremony to welcome the ponies every time they returned. But now my people have forgotten the old ways. Many no longer believe the legend. They do not pay honor to the Appaloosas. They do not care that the ponies are in danger."

"What kind of danger?" Billy asked.

5

"There are still white men who want the ponies. They rope them and take them away. Each year the herd grows smaller. If this is not stopped, one day there will be no more of the great ponies."

"Gosh!" Billy exclaimed. "I'd better tell Pa about this."

"No," Concha said softly, but firmly. "This is only for you and me to know."

"If that's what you want," Billy agreed.

"It is the way it must be," Concha insisted.

Although Billy wanted to know why Concha had told him about the plight of the ponies, he knew better than to ask more questions. He knew that Concha had told him as much as he wanted him to know.

Billy turned and watched the ponies as they grazed in the meadow. As the sun lowered to the crest of the western canyon, the golden light shimmered on the backs of the Appaloosas. How peaceful they seemed. It was hard to believe that anyone would want to harm these beautiful animals. But Billy knew that Concha always spoke the truth.

Chapter 3

An Overheard Conversation

The next few days were exciting ones for Billy. His mother and father held a horse sale. It was Billy's job to hand out leaflets to the buyers, so they would have a list of the names and prices of all the horses.

On the last day of the sale, Billy happened to notice two men dressed in blue jeans and cotton shirts. One was wearing a dingy blue cowboy hat. The other man had a droopy red hat on his head.

Most of the people at the sale were neighbors, so Billy knew them. But he had never seen the two strangers. He noticed the man wearing the blue hat was large and powerful looking. The one with the red hat was thin and wiry.

In the afternoon, Billy overheard a conversation between the two men.

"Them horses are too dang expensive!" the big man said.

"But, Hollis, we *must* get at least two of 'em!" argued the other one.

Then Hollis grinned a kind of grin that made Billy feel uneasy. The boy knew the men were up to no good, so he edged closer to listen.

"Hey, Will, do you remember them ponies out by the meadow?" Hollis smiled.

"You mean the Appaloosas?" Will said.

"Exactly," Hollis answered, and his smile grew broader.

"All right, Hollis," Will chuckled, "what are you hatching up in that evil mind of yours?"

"Just you wait and see," Hollis said.

Flashes of horrible things the men might do to the ponies streaked through Billy's mind. He remembered what Concha had told him about people who would try to capture the ponies. He also remembered that he had promised himself to help the ponies if they were ever in trouble. Now might be that time.

Trying not to draw attention, Billy moved through the crowd of buyers, looking for Concha. When Billy finally found Concha, he told him what he had overheard and pointed toward the men.

Concha's face tightened thoughtfully. "Be still, Billy," he whispered. "Don't look their way again. We do not want them to know we have found out anything. But we must help the ponies."

"How?" Billy wondered aloud, looking down and shaking his head.

But Concha didn't answer. When Billy looked up, the old Indian had disappeared into the crowd.

Chapter 4

Where Are the Ponies?

Billy wondered why Concha had left him so suddenly. He also wondered how he could save the ponies. And although the boy wanted to, he didn't tell his father or mother about the two men. He knew Concha wouldn't want him to tell anyone.

The next morning, Billy rode Ginger out to the meadow. When he saw the Appaloosas were not there, he shivered with fright. But when he rode down into the valley a little farther, he was relieved to find the ponies peacefully grazing.

Billy was sad to think the Appaloosas would soon be leaving for Arizona, but he realized that the sooner they left, the safer they would be. He hoped they would go before those men had a chance to try something.

Suddenly Billy saw Concha walking toward him.

"Concha, why did you leave the sale in such a hurry yesterday?" Billy wanted to know.

Concha did not answer the boy's question. Instead, he replied, "The ponies will soon need your help."

"But how can *I* help them?" Billy asked anxiously.

"When the time comes, you will know what to do," Concha promised. Then the old Indian turned and walked away.

Billy did not understand. Now he was more disturbed than ever.

That night at supper, Billy's mother noticed he looked worried.

"What's bothering you, Billy?" she asked.

"Oh, nothing. I'm just thinking," Billy answered slowly.

At dawn the next morning, Billy dressed quickly. He hurried with his chores, because he was eager to ride out to the meadow. He grabbed a sack of oatmeal cookies his mother had baked and stopped at the well to fill his canteen with water. Then he strapped a saddle on Ginger and climbed on.

"Billy, where are you going?" his mother called.

"Oh, just to the meadow to watch the Appaloosa ponies," he replied."

"Well, don't be late for supper!" she ordered.

"Yes, Ma," Billy nodded, as he urged Ginger into a gallop.

This morning Billy rode past the meadow and into the valley, but he could not find the ponies anywhere. He wondered if the Appaloosas had started toward Arizona. He hoped they had. But then he began to fear that the two men had already captured the ponies and taken them away.

Billy had to find out!

Chapter 5

The Chase

Billy rode Ginger farther and farther into the valley. He continued to look for the herd of ponies, but they were nowhere to be found. So he started out across the plains.

About noon Billy slowed Ginger to a walk. He finally stopped his horse by a grove of trees. Climbing down, he took a long drink from his canteen. Then he poured water into his cupped hand and gave Ginger a drink too.

Just as Billy started to take a bite of cookie, he heard voices in the distance. Eating was forgotten. He quickly tied Ginger to a bush, then quietly...ever so quietly...he crept through the underbrush.

As Billy edged closer, the voices became louder. Then he saw the two men — Hollis and Will. So Billy crept even closer and hid behind a bush.

"We've followed them ponies long enough," Billy heard Hollis say. "Let's sneak up on 'em and drive 'em into that dead-end canyon, just south of here. Then we'll have 'em!"

Billy quietly returned to Ginger and climbed into the saddle. He waited until Will and Hollis had ridden about a quarter mile, then he followed them. For almost an hour, Billy stalked the two men as they stalked the ponies.

When a rabbit suddenly darted between Ginger's feet, the mare shied and whinnied in alarm. Crack! Snap! Twigs and sagebrush rustled and popped all around Billy and his horse.

Hearing the sounds, the men whirled their horses around and saw Billy.

Thinking quickly, the boy moved Ginger into a fast gallop, rode past the two startled horse thieves and headed straight for the Appaloosas.

"Oh, no!" Billy said aloud. "They're heading into the dead-end canyon! The ponies will be trapped! And I'll be trapped too!"

Billy looked back over his shoulder to see if Will and Hollis were following him. They were!

At this point, Billy could have turned Ginger around and headed for safety, but he wouldn't leave the ponies. He didn't know how he could help them, but he knew he had to at least try.

So on he rode — straight into the canyon!

Chapter 6

A Passage

Billy was frantic! Knowing he must warn the Appaloosas, he spurred his horse on. As he raced toward the ponies, he began flapping his hat in the wind.

"Get out of the canyon!" he yelled. "Run, or you'll be trapped!"

But the ponies didn't run. Instead, they turned and looked calmly at Billy. They just stood there as if they were waiting for him.

By the time Billy reached the ponies, Hollis and Will were not far behind. So the boy rode right into the midst of the ponies. Bending forward, he pressed his stomach close to Ginger's back, hoping that he could hide among the Appaloosas.

Then the strangest thing happened. The afternoon sky turned as black as night. Billy couldn't see anything. He heard Hollis and Will's horses galloping toward him at full speed. Then — Wham! He heard their horses hit the side of the canyon wall. And he heard the men cry out as they were thrown hard against the rocks. After that all was quiet, except for the soft howling of the wind.

Then something even stranger happened. Suddenly a blazing beam of light burst forth from the wall of the canyon. The light grew brighter and brighter. It became so intense that Billy was almost blinded.

Ginger whinnied with fear and shied backward. But Billy refused to look away. Determined to see the source of the brightness, he squinted his eyes and looked deep into the center of the glowing light.

And then he saw it — only a flickering image at first, but then it moved and tossed its head from side to side. And with a thrust of power, it reared up on its hind legs, and the sound of its whinnying echoed throughout the canyon.

Standing in the center of the light was a mighty Appaloosa — the Great White Stallion!

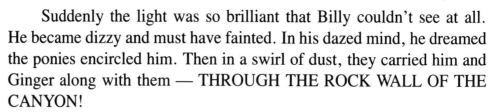

Suddenly the light was so brilliant that Billy couldn't see at all. He became dizzy and must have fainted. In his dazed mind, he dreamed the ponies encircled him. Then in a swirl of dust, they carried him and Ginger along with them — THROUGH THE ROCK WALL OF THE CANYON!

Billy and Ginger, and all of the ponies, seemed to float on beams of light, as the Great White Stallion led them through a giant cavern of winding passages. When they came out on the other side of the wall, they were in a deep valley.

Millions of bright stars twinkled overhead. Surrounded in the brilliant light, the Great White Stallion blazed a path toward the stars. And Billy watched as the mighty Appaloosa disappeared into the night sky.

Billy awoke from his startling dream to find he was still in the valley — the most beautiful, peaceful valley he had ever seen. Moonlight as clear and warm as sunlight illuminated fresh green meadows and brightly colored flowers. A waterfall, streaked with silver moonlight, poured into a glistening pool.

The thirsty ponies stood by the pool, drinking their fill. Billy watched as Ginger joined them.

Realizing he was thirsty too, Billy reached for his canteen, but he couldn't find it. Deciding he must have dropped it in the canyon, he walked to the pool, and lying flat on his stomach, he drank from the cool water. It was the most refreshing water he had ever tasted. As he relaxed, the friendly Appaloosas nuzzled their warm noses against him.

During the night, Billy thought about the day's adventures. He thought about the Great White Stallion that had stood in the center of the light. He wondered if the stallion was one of the ancient herd. Had the mighty horse led them into a hidden passage or had he spirited them through solid rock? Billy didn't know, and he began to wonder if he had dreamed the whole thing.

Will and Hollis didn't know what had happened either. When they woke up, they were terribly bruised all over and had bumps on their heads. In a state of shock, Will was babbling something about "horses disappearing into the wall."

"Don't be a fool," growled Hollis, standing up and brushing the dirt from his clothing. "You don't know what you're talking about. You just hit your head when you fell off your horse. Just look at that bump on your noggin."

18

"But I *saw* them!" Will insisted.

"You're just loco," Will grumbled. "While we were out cold, them ponies turned around and ran back out of the canyon. They're probably halfway to Arizona by now."

"I know what I saw!" Will insisted, as he grabbed up a canteen lying on the ground beside him. He opened the canteen and poured its last drops of cool water over his aching head.

"Wonder who this canteen belongs to?" Will said. "You know, I'll bet it belongs to that kid. And I'll bet *he* rode through that canyon wall too!"

"Stop imagining things!" Hollis ordered.

In disgust Will tossed the empty canteen to the ground and looked toward the canyon wall. All he saw was a solid sheet of rock.

"There ain't enough space for a snake to slither through," Will said, "but somehow them horses kept right on goin'. I seen it and you did too!"

"I never want to see them ponies again," Hollis finally said. "If there's something weird goin' on here, I don't want no part of it. Let's head north, and fast."

And as soon as Will and Hollis found their horses, that's exactly what they did.

Chapter 7

Free

When Billy awoke the next morning, he was surprised to find himself back in the canyon with Ginger and the Appaloosas.

His adventures had made him hungry. So he reached into his pocket for the cookies and gobbled them down. Now he was thirsty, so he started looking for his canteen. He remembered it still had a little water inside.

"Thank goodness!" he said when he saw it.

He scooped up the canteen, opened it, and took a couple of gulps of water — cool, cool water that reminded him of the water in the pool.

Suddenly he stopped drinking and looked at the canteen. He shook it and heard the water sloshing around inside — not just a little water, but a lot of water.

"That's strange. How could there still be so much water inside?" Billy wondered aloud.

The boy drank some more. Then he turned to look at the canyon wall. He shook his head in disbelief. Before him there was nothing but solid rock.

Then Billy heard the restless hooves of the ponies, as they pawed the ground. He watched as the Appaloosas began to run back and forth in excitement. When one pony took the lead and started toward the southern plains, all the others followed.

A very thoughtful Billy watched the Appaloosas leave on their yearly trip. He could not explain everything that had happened. But he knew the ponies were now safe and that somehow he had helped save

them from being captured. Satisfied with what he had done, Billy walked over to Ginger and climbed into the saddle. He rode out of the canyon and across the plains toward home.

In the afternoon, Billy saw the familiar outline of the ranch house. He encouraged Ginger to gallop a little faster, and they were soon home.

Billy's mother and father were overjoyed to see him.

"When you didn't come home last night, we were so worried!" his mother said, hugging him.

"You'd be in trouble, young man," his father said, "if Concha hadn't come by to tell us you were safe with the Appaloosas."

"Oh, Pa!" Billy said excitedly. "You should have been there! It was like magic! I saw the Great White Stallion of the Appaloosas!"

Billy's parents listened as he told them of his strange adventure. He told them about the bright light and how he and Ginger and the ponies raced through the canyon wall.

Billy's mother and father wanted to believe their son's story, but they couldn't help but wonder whether the boy's imagination had gotten the best of him.

Later in the afternoon, Billy rode Ginger to the meadow. Somehow he knew that Concha would be waiting for him. When he saw the old Indian, Billy dismounted and ran to tell his friend about all he had seen.

"It was the most beautiful thing I ever saw!" Billy exclaimed. "The wall opened like magic. Oh, Concha, you do believe me, don't you?"

Concha smiled and nodded his head. "I believe you, Billy. I know you speak the truth," he said. "I know, because I was with you."

Billy looked up into the face of his friend. Seeing the sunlight glistening on Concha's snow-white hair, the boy could not help but notice that it was as white as the coat of the Great Appaloosa Stallion.

1987 WINNERS

Dennis Vollmer

Lisa Gross

Stacy Chbosky

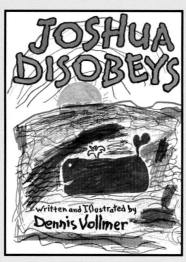

Amy Hagstrom

Joshua Disobeys
written and illustrated by
Dennis Vollmer, age 6
winner of the 6-9 Age Category

Although Joshua's mother warns him not to go near the shore, the baby whale disobeys and becomes "beached."

Dennis skillfully tells of Joshua's misadventures and of the young boy who tries to help him. With a marvelous sense of design and an extraordinary display of overlaying colors, Dennis's amazing illustrations are absolute delights.

Hardcover
In Full Color   ISBN 0-933849-12-5

The Half & Half Dog
written and illustrated by
Lisa Gross, age 12
winner of the 10-13 Age Category

One half of the half-and-half dog is Scottie, the other half is golden retriever. Because of his unusual appearance, he is laughed at and ridiculed. The half-and-half dog's search for acceptance and the discovery of his self-esteem is a touching and often hilarious story. Lisa's wonderful illustrations are colorful delights.

Hardcover
In Full Color   ISBN 0-933849-13-3

Who Owns the Sun
written and illustrated by
Stacy Chbosky, age 14
winner of the 14-19 Age Category

With full-color impressionistic illustra-tions and a flow of narrative that tran forms prose into poetry, Stacy unleashe a powerful story and a plaintive cry f freedom. In her extraordinary book, sh gently affects the mind and heart, as sh touches an essential part of the huma spirit and creates a meaningful exper ence for readers of all ages.

Hardcover
In Full Color   ISBN 0-933849-14-

1986 WINNERS

Isaac Whitlatch

Dav Pilkey

Strong and Free
written and illustrated by
Amy Hagstrom, age 9
winner of the 6-9 Age Category

When a herd of wild Appaloosas is threatened, a young boy and an old In-dian try to save the ponies from capture. An exciting journey leads them to a lost canyon and to the unforgettable mystical vision of the Great White Stallion.

Amy's skillfully written narrative weaves an Indian legend into a modern adven-ture. Her lovely sponge-print illustrations are breathtakingly beautiful.

Hardcover
In Full Color   ISBN 0-933849-08-7

Me and My Veggies
written and illustrated by
Isaac Whitlatch, age 11
winner of the 10-13 Age Category

The true confessions of a devout veg-etable hater are told tongue-in-cheek by a boy who has met the enemy, spoonful by spoonful, and won. Isaac relates his madcap misadventures and offers read-ers surefire strategies for avoiding and disposing of the "slimy green things." His delightful color illustrations and his rib-tickling prose serve readers a finely chopped salad of laughter and mirth.

Hardcover
In Full Color   ISBN 0-933849-09-5

World War Won
written and illustrated by
Dav Pilkey, age 19
winner of the 14-19 Age Category

When two kings, a fox and a raccoor become embroiled in an arms race, eac tries to build the tallest stockpile of wea ons. When they realize their towers powers could blow the world to smith ereens, they work together in a searc for peace. This timely parable, presente with humor and thought-provoking i sight, offers hope for universal peace ar understanding. It's a real winner!

Hardcover
In Full Color   ISBN 0-933849-10-

Winning Students' Books Entertain, Inform and Motivate!

Books for students, written and illustrated by students. What a wonderful idea! Our school has them all in its library, but the books are seldom on the shelf.

My students are fascinated with these books and so am I. The subjects are varied and popular, the illustrations are superb and eye catching, and the reading levels are suited to the subjects. Each student's book, chosen from among thousands submitted for the Contest, can stand uniquely on its own merit in full competition with books written and illustrated by adults.

But more than that, each book is an invitation, a challenge to the reader that he or she too can write and illustrate such a book. My students like to read about the authors and imagine what winning the contest means to them. No better motivation can be found for inspiring students to write creatively or for encouraging them to read.

Better still — these are very good books that will withstand the test of time. They will remain popular years from now. With the finest of editing and customized printing provided to complement the story line and illustrations for each book, it seems safe to predict that future additions to this series will repeat the outstanding quality so evident in present winners.

So upon receiving the prepublication announcement, I confidently order the new winners and, like my students, I can hardly wait to read the books when they arrive.

May Landmark continue to produce these students' wonderful books for many years to come.

Marge Hagerty, Library Media Specialist
Park Hill District, Kansas City, Missouri

To obtain Contest Rules, send a self-addressed, stamped, business-size envelope to: THE NATIONAL WRITTEN & ILLUSTRATED BY... AWARDS CONTEST FOR STUDENTS, Landmark Editions, Inc., P.O. Box 4469, Kansas City, MO 64127

Landmark 1985 Gold Award Books

Before initiating The National Written & Illustrated by... Awards Contest for Students, Landmark published two students' books — WALKING IS WILD, WEIRD AND WACKY and THE DRAGON OF ORD. Both books were immediate hits with teachers and students.

I read DRAGON and WALKING to my class and they just loved them! *All they wanted to do was draw, draw, draw, and write, write, write!* **Rhonda Pierce, Teacher**

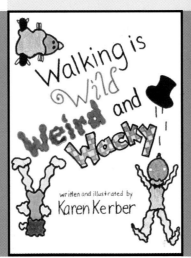

Karen Kerber

David McAdoo

Walking Is Wild, Weird and Wacky
written and illustrated by
Karen Kerber, age 12

A delightful picture book, filled with gentle humor and playful alliteration. Karen's brightly colored illustrations offer wiggly and waggly strokes of genius!

Hardcover
Printed in Full Color ISBN 0-933849-01-X

The Dragon of Ord
written and illustrated by
David McAdoo, age 14

An intergalactic adventure, hurling space ships into the future and forcing a final confrontation between the hero and the monstrous Dragon of Ord. David's heroic narrative is exciting and full of action. His skills as an illustrator are astounding!

Hardcover
Printed in Duotone ISBN 0-933849-02-8

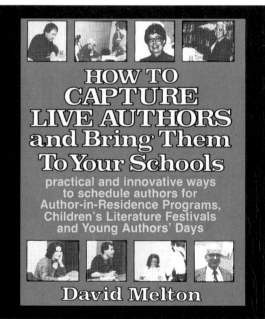